D0499721

Learning to Read, Step by Step!

Ready to Read   Preschool–Kindergarten
• big type and easy words • rhyme and rhythm • picture clues
For children who know the alphabet and are eager to
begin reading.

Reading with Help   Preschool–Grade 1
• basic vocabulary • short sentences • simple stories
For children who recognize familiar words and sound out
new words with help.

Reading on Your Own   Grades 1–3
• engaging characters • easy-to-follow plots • popular topics
For children who are ready to read on their own.

Reading Paragraphs   Grades 2–3
• challenging vocabulary • short paragraphs • exciting stories
For newly independent readers who read simple sentences
with confidence.

Ready for Chapters   Grades 2–4
• chapters • longer paragraphs • full-color art
For children who want to take the plunge into chapter books
but still like colorful pictures.

STEP INTO READING® is designed to give every child a successful
reading experience. The grade levels are only guides; children will progress
through the steps at their own speed, developing confidence in their reading.

Remember, a lifetime love of reading starts with a single step!

Visit us on the Web!
StepIntoReading.com
rhcbooks.com

Educators and librarians, for a variety of teaching tools, visit us at
RHTeachersLibrarians.com

ISBN 978-1-101-93911-6 (trade) — ISBN 978-1-101-93912-3 (lib. bdg.) — ISBN 978-1-101-93913-0 (ebook)

Printed in the United States of America
10 9 8 7 6 5 4 3 2 1

WILD KRATTS®

Wild Fliers!

by Martin Kratt and Chris Kratt

Random House 🏠 New York

Have you ever wished
that you could fly?
Us too!

That's why we love
to learn about
amazing animals
with the ability to fly.

The Secrets of Flight

All animals that fly have a special feature: wings!

Birds have wings
with feathers.
Insects are small and
have wings made of chitin
(pronounced kite-en).

The Fastest Flier!

Peregrine falcons are
the fastest fliers in the world.
They fly high looking for
birds to chase—and eat!

When the falcon spots
its prey, it tucks in
its wings and drops.
This is called a stoop.
The Peregrine falcon can
reach speeds of about
200 miles per hour!

The Long-Distance Fliers

Monarch butterflies are beautiful insects with delicate wings.

But they are tough, too.

Every year monarch
butterflies fly
for thousands of miles.
It's a long trip called
a migration.

The Long-Distance Fliers

Many birds migrate as well.
Canada geese fly south
for the winter.
They have powerful chest
muscles that keep their
wide wings flapping.

They fly together in
a group shaped like a V.
They honk to keep
the group together.

The Hoverers

Hummingbirds can flap
their wings 80 times
a second!
This allows them to hover,
or stay in one spot,
in the air!

Hummingbirds can fly forward and backward– and even upside down! They hover to sip nectar from flowers.

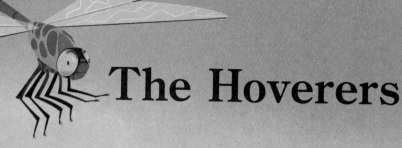

The Hoverers

Dragonflies can hover, too.
They use their flying
powers to hunt insects . . .

and escape predators!

The Swervy Fliers

Purple martins are
amazing fliers.
They swerve and swoop
as they hunt insects:
moths, mosquitoes,
and mayflies.

Mammal Fliers

Bats are mammals that fly.
Little brown bats twist
and turn in the air while
they chase insects to eat.

Their wings are like hands with skin stretched between the long fingers.

The Gliders

Gliders don't really fly.
They jump and spread
their "wings" to take off!

A draco lizard jumps
from a tree and glides
to another tree.

Flying fish jump
out of the water
and glide on wide fins
to escape from dolphins.
They can glide for
over two hundred yards.

The Non-Fliers

Penguins are birds that cannot fly in the air. Their bodies and wings are adapted to swimming!

Penguins swim
to catch fish and escape
hungry predators,
like leopard seals.

Soaring Fliers

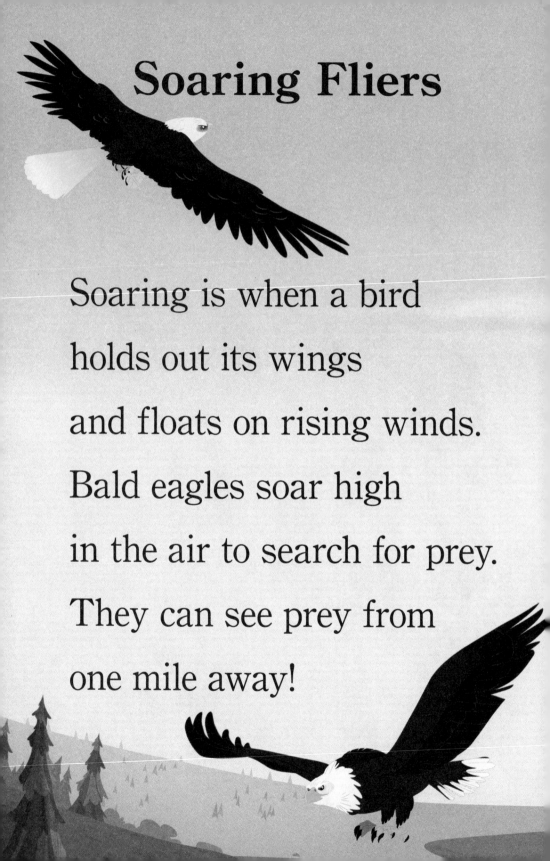

Soaring is when a bird
holds out its wings
and floats on rising winds.
Bald eagles soar high
in the air to search for prey.
They can see prey from
one mile away!

Turkey vultures are great
at soaring, too.
They use both smell
and sight to search
for food.

So Many Fliers

There are over one million
types of flying insects
in the world!
There are more than
ten thousand types of
flying birds!

And there are more than one thousand types of bats!

Which one is your favorite wild flier?

The Kratt Brothers agree—
with so many fantastic
wild fliers, it is very hard
to choose.

Let's fly!